First published in 2021 in Great Britain by
Barrington Stoke Ltd
18 Walker Street, Edinburgh, EH3 7LP

www.barringtonstoke.co.uk

Text © 2021 Pip Jones
Illustrations © 2021 Paula Bowles

A CIP catalogue record for this book is available
from the British Library upon request

ISBN: 978-1-78112-951-7

Printed by Hussar Books, Poland

This book is in a super-readable format for young readers
beginning their independent reading journey.

MADAM SQUEAKER

PIP JONES

Illustrated by
Paula Bowles

Barrington Stoke

*For my beautiful niece Martha,
for my sister Katie, and for mighty
girls and women everywhere. xx*

CONTENTS

1. Half a peanut and a speck of cheese   1

2. Scratching and screeching   6

3. A terrible mess   11

4. Some Sage advice   19

5. "Find your voice!"   25

6. The teacup   30

7. To the loft!   37

8. No room for a mouse   42

9. Coo! Coo!   51

10. Minetta makes a plan   60

11. Stepping out from the shadows   65

12. Order!   77

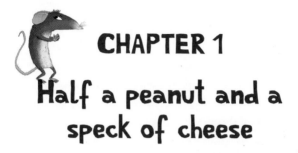

CHAPTER 1

Half a peanut and a speck of cheese

The garden around Hollyhock House shone in the evening sun. Inside the creaking old building, Minetta Squeaker, a tiny grey-brown mouse, had found a lovely cool spot under the bottom step in the hall. It was the perfect place to eat her evening meal.

"Billy?" Minetta squeaked. "Won't you come and sit with me?"

Billy the spider opened three of her eyes and looked down from her cobweb. "Sorry, Minetta. What did you say? I didn't hear you."

"Come and sit with me while I eat!" Minetta squeaked louder.

"It's not worth coming down!" Billy yawned. "That's not much of a dinner, Minetta. It'll all be gone in three bites!"

Billy was right – Minetta didn't have much to eat tonight. She had only found a few scraps dropped by the Two Legs who lived in the house – three cracker crumbs, a speck of cheddar cheese and half a peanut.

"I'll just have to make the most of it," Minetta said, and she popped the cheese in her mouth. "Perhaps I'll have more luck tomorrow."

"Not with those rats about!" Billy scoffed. "They never leave anything for anyone else to eat if they can help it."

CHAPTER 2
Scratching and screeching

Thinking about the rats made Minetta's fur stand on end.

In a house this big, with so many Two Legs living in it, there should have been plenty of food to go around, if only the rats would share it out.

Minetta's tummy rumbled. She'd seen a delicious cake in the kitchen that afternoon. It must have been the littlest Two Legs' birthday, because Minetta had watched him blow out five sparkling candles while the others sang a happy song.

A cake like that would leave lots of lovely crumbs, but Minetta hadn't had any.

The rats got there first, just like they always did. Whenever the Two Legs weren't looking, the rats zoomed in and took whatever they wanted – and the little mice went hungry, day after day.

Minetta gave a sigh. She finished her peanut and waited quietly, listening.

Creak! Creak!

She heard the creak of the stairs and then:

Click! Click!

The click of doors meant the Two Legs had gone upstairs to their beds. Soon after came the scratching and screeching and scampering feet.

The rats were coming down from the loft.

CHAPTER 3

A terrible mess

Minetta peeped through a crack in the step as the rats ran down the stairs, their paws thundering on the wood.

Bandit was the biggest rat of all. He had a pointy face and an evil grin. "Come on!" he shouted. "Let's have some fun!"

His friends – Trixie, Hoover and Fink – cackled with glee as all the rats ran straight to the kitchen. Minetta rushed after them, just in time to see one of the Two Legs' teacups crash to the floor. The bottom of it broke right off.

"Those ratty rat faces!" came a whisper from a dark corner. "They think they can do anything they like!"

It was Minetta's mouse friend, Tan. Tan shook his head and tutted as the rats darted along the kitchen tops and gobbled up anything they found left over from the Two Legs' dinner.

Soon there wasn't a crumb left anywhere.

"To the garden!" Bandit shouted, diving through the cat flap. "We'll eat all the peas tonight!"

"Easy-PEASY!" Hoover sniggered.

"The peas?" Minetta squealed. "It will be another two weeks before they are ripe! Please leave them, then *all of us* can have a lovely, sweet pea *each* at the end of the month!"

But the rats didn't hear Minetta. They pushed rudely past her and scurried out to the vegetable patch

where they began ripping off the pea
pods with their teeth.

Minetta scampered out after them
and watched sadly. The rats were
making a terrible mess and there would
be no juicy peas for anyone else.

Suddenly, from above, came a
SWOOSH!

Wings! Huge shining eyes! An open beak!

Minetta hid under a dandelion leaf and squeaked in fright.

"Oh, no! An *owl*!"

CHAPTER 4
Some Sage advice

The owl landed on the handle of a garden fork.

She looked down slowly at Minetta, who was trembling.

"You needn't be afraid, mouse," the owl said. "I've had my supper and, anyway, you're a bit too thin and bony for me."

Minetta slowly stepped out from behind her leaf.

"I can't help being thin and bony," she sighed.

"So I see," said the owl, looking at the rats as they guzzled up all the peas. "My name is Sage. Who are you?"

"I'm Min-Min-etta Squeaker!" Minetta stuttered.

"Good evening, Minetta," said Sage. "I've come to give you some advice."

"Oh, thank you!" said Minetta. "I've heard that owls are very wise."

"Those rotten rats over there are ruling the roost!" Sage said. "I hear them

talking at night when I rest on the roof.
They don't just want to take all the Two
Legs' leftover food. They want the house,
too."

"The house?"

Behind Sage, Trixie was chasing a
hedgehog away from the vegetable patch,
where it had been rooting for worms.

"The rats want Hollyhock House and this garden all to themselves," Sage continued. "They plan to send all of you – the mice, the hedgehogs, the doves and everyone else – out to The Bogland."

CHAPTER 5

"Find your voice!"

Minetta clapped her paws to her mouth in horror. Did the rats really want to get rid of her and all her friends?

She'd heard The Bogland was a terrible place. Cold, wet and sticky with mud, the bog could just swallow little animals up if they didn't watch out. Minetta really didn't want to go there.

"What can we do?" the mouse asked, her eyes shining with worry.

"You need to stand up to them, Minetta!"

"Me?"

"Yes, why not you?"

"I'm so … small!"

Sage's head feathers twitched.

"We are only as small as we let others make us feel," Sage said. "Inside you is a speck of courage. Let it grow and you might find you have a very big voice indeed. Perhaps the rats and your friends will listen!"

SWOOSH!

Sage took off, but before she flew past the lowest branch of the oak tree, she called back:

"Find your voice, Minetta! I'll be listening!"

CHAPTER 6

The teacup

Minetta left the rats wrecking the garden and went back to the kitchen.

As she sat thinking about what Sage the owl had said, she spotted the Two Legs' broken teacup.

"Perhaps I could fix it for them!" she said out loud.

Tan was still there in the shadows. "Come on," he said. "I'll help you take it back to your hole."

"I prefer to call it my 'home', Tan."

"All right, your home!" he laughed as they picked up the two pieces of china.

The teacup didn't fit through the crack that was Minetta's front door, so they had to go home the long way round – via the cupboard under the staircase and through the gap where the hot water pipes clanked and gurgled.

At last they were there and Minetta flopped down on her bed, tired after all the effort.

"So, what can we glue it with?" asked Tan. "I thought I saw a pot of honey on a shelf in the kitchen the other day. Mmm, honey is *lovely* and sticky!"

"If you got your paws in the honey pot, I don't think you'd use the honey for glue!" Minetta giggled. "It would all end up in here!"

She poked his fluffy tummy and he squeaked loudly.

"I don't think honey would work anyway, Tan," Minetta went on. "I'll have to try to find some proper glue. In the meantime, I need to *do* something about those rats.

"Sage told me they want to scare us all away from our lovely home. They must be back up in the loft by now. Perhaps I just need to go and talk to them."

"You can't go up to the loft!" Tan gasped.

"Yes, I can. Come with me, Tan!" Minetta whispered. "It'll be an adventure!"

CHAPTER 7

To the loft!

The staircase loomed in front of Minetta
and Tan like a mountain.

"I've never been upstairs," Tan
whispered. "We don't even know what's
up there."

"The RATS are up there!" Minetta
replied. "And the loft is right at the top,

so we just have to keep going up, up, up until we find them."

Minetta climbed the first step and Tan followed. They soon found it was fun scrambling up the steps one by one and zigzagging through the banisters.

Before too long, and ever so out of breath, they saw there were no more steps to climb.

That meant they were at the top.

In the loft.

In front of them was a door and behind the door were the rats.

Minetta and Tan pressed their round ears to the thick wooden door to listen.

"I can't hear properly!" Minetta whispered. "We'll have to have to sneak inside."

Before Tan could argue, Minetta
had pressed her body flat against the
floorboards and slipped right under the
door.

Tan held his breath, then did the
same.

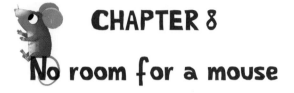

CHAPTER 8
No room for a mouse

From a dark corner of the loft, Minetta and Tan watched and listened. The rats were seated round a huge plank of wood that was covered with food.

There were broken crackers, whole bread crusts and a huge pile of peanuts. Tan gasped when he spotted the upturned honey pot.

"Do NOT let it rumble!" Minetta whispered, poking his tummy.

"WE ARE THE RULING RATS!" Bandit chanted, bashing his fists on the table.

The other rats copied him: "We are the Ruling Rats! We are the Ruling Rats!"

"Why should we share?"

"We just don't care!"

"OUR food and OUR house!"

"No room for a mouse!"

"Those silly little mice!"

"They should take our advice!"

"AND GO TO LIVE IN THE BOGLAND!"

Minetta had heard enough.

"Hello! Hello?" she squeaked. "We are mice from downstairs and we need to speak to you!"

The rats didn't hear her tiny voice over all their shouting.

None of them even looked over in her direction, and the horrible jeering, laughing and sneering rang through the rafters.

"Hey, Tan?" Minetta whispered, frowning. "Where are all the doves? Doves have always been allowed to roost

up here in the loft – even the Two Legs liked them."

"They've gone," Tan sighed. "The rats ordered the doves to bring them more and more berries, and when they didn't bring enough, the rats made them leave."

Minetta's fur stood on end in anger. But then, above the rickety roof tiles, she felt sure she heard a noise she knew:

SWOOSH!

It was the wings of an owl.

CHAPTER 9

Coo! Coo!

Back in her house under the stairs, Minetta groaned. "This is terrible!" she said. "The rats have everything and now the doves have nothing! Where will they go? The doves are hatching more chicks this month – how will they be safe?"

"If we speak to the doves," said Tan, "maybe they can help us try to talk to the rats again."

"But we don't know where the doves have gone!" Minetta cried. "They could be far, far away."

"What was that you said?" Billy yawned and turned in her cobweb to hear.

"I said, I don't know where the doves are," Minetta repeated.

"I still can't hear you! Speak louder," said Billy.

Minetta huffed, then leaned forwards to shout.

"THE DOVES!" she yelled as loudly as she could. "I NEED TO SEE THE DOVES!"

This time, Minetta's voice echoed right through the broken teacup. The sound boomed out from under the stair, right around the hall, and even made the letter box rattle.

Billy swung in her cobweb, shocked.

"All right, all right!" she cried. "I heard you that time!"

Minetta was about to tell Billy all about what they had seen up in the loft when another sound came from outside.

"Coo! Coo!"

"What was that?" Tan gasped.

"*I think I heard a dove!*" squeaked Minetta.

Minetta and Tan dashed out from under the step, scampered across the hall and slid under the front door.

Covering the lawn in front of Hollyhock House were the doves, all twenty of them.

"Did you call, Minetta?" asked Atticus, a pink-grey dove with an elegant black collar.

"Atticus!" Minetta cried. "You heard me! Gosh, I *am* pleased to see you all. We have things to talk about. We need to make a plan."

CHAPTER 10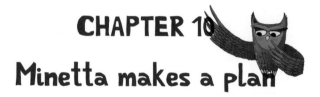
Minetta makes a plan

Minetta was up early the next day.

"Good morning!"

She shouted it through the teacup to wake Billy the spider up.

Billy's eyes snapped open.

"Not so loud!" she complained. "You and that noisy teacup ruined my lovely dream!"

"Yes, well, I've been thinking about this teacup," Minetta said. "I'm going to keep it, just for a little while. I have a feeling it might be useful up in the loft!"

"So, what was the plan you made with the doves?" Billy asked, swinging down on her thread.

Minetta smiled. "Today, Tan and I are going to round up all the mice from every corner of Hollyhock House. The doves are going to get their new chicks to bed early and then we're all going up to the loft together. We're going to *make* the rats listen."

Tan squeezed in through the crack.

"Ready?" he asked.

"Ready!" Minetta said. "You start in the basement and I'll start on the second floor, then we'll meet in the middle. When we've spoken to all the mice, we'll wait till the sun goes down, then find the hedgehogs and voles in the garden."

"It's going to be a busy day!" Tan called, scampering away.

It is, thought Minetta to herself, tapping the teacup. *I think I might have found my voice!*

CHAPTER 11

Stepping out from the shadows

Late that evening, when Minetta was sure the rats had gone to the garden, she led all the small animals up the stairs to the top of the house.

The rats had left the door open, so Minetta and her friends rushed in to the loft room, just as the doves flew in through the gaps in the rafters.

Atticus swooped down and placed Minetta's teacup carefully at the end of the long plank table.

"Thank you!" Minetta squeaked.

"No problem!" Atticus called as he flew up to perch on a beam. "It would have taken you ages to drag that heavy teacup up all those stairs!"

Through the open window, the little animals heard the rats far below in the garden, digging up the baby carrots and chomping them noisily.

"Wait in the shadows," Minetta told her friends. "The rats will be back soon."

The little mouse sat at the end of
the table and put her paw on the teacup.
Then she waited for the thundering of rat
paws up the stairs.

Bandit was the first rat through the
door.

"Who are YOU?" he yelled when he
saw Minetta. "Get lost, little mouse!
We are the Ruling Rats and this is *our*
house!"

"Why is that rat so small?" Fink whispered.

"It's a *mouse*," Hoover whispered back, rolling his eyes.

"Chase it out!" screeched Trixie.

Bandit lunged towards Minetta, but he jumped back when 124 of her friends stepped out of the shadows or flew down from the rafters.

The rats began booing and shouting. Trixie leaned on Tan and snarled.

Minetta picked up her teacup.

"We will NOT be chased away!" she shouted. "Stop bullying the smaller animals of Hollyhock House. We can all live here together in a way that is fair to everyone!"

This time the rats *did* hear Minetta and they yelled and shrieked and waved their fists.

"You can't tell us what to do!" Bandit scoffed.

SWOOSH!

"She most certainly can!" came a booming voice from the window.

Everyone turned to see who had spoken and suddenly all the arguing stopped.

Perched on the windowsill was Sage.

CHAPTER 12

Order!

Sage glared at wide-eyed Bandit, who gave a large "Gulp!"

A few of the mice squeaked.

"It's OK," Minetta whispered. "Sage is my friend."

She picked up her teacup again. "From today, every animal or bird at Hollyhock House will have a place at this table. Together we will make the rules for living fairly and in peace!"

"It is called a parliament," Sage said.

"A parly-what?" Bandit snapped.

"A parliament. We owls have *always* had a parliament."

The rats began to roar and jeer all over again. The mice squeaked back. The doves, voles and hedgehogs cooed, grunted and argued until ...

"Order!" Minetta boomed. "We will have order in this house!"

Minetta had shouted so loudly and
with such determination that this time
everyone hushed and looked at her.
Some of the rats even shook a little.

Tan grinned and pointed at Minetta's
paw.

When she looked down, Minetta
was astonished. She wasn't holding the
teacup!

"I see that you have found your voice," Sage said proudly, then turned to the rats. "All of you here will give Minetta the respect she deserves. You will listen when she speaks. You will speak when she says it is your turn and from now on you will call her Madam Squeaker."

Tan and the other mice cheered. Bandit sighed and nodded. It was no good – he knew that Minetta and her friends were right.

Minetta smiled her thanks to the owl, who opened her wings and with one

SWOOSH!

vanished into the night.

Minetta gave a little cough.

"The first thing we need to talk about," she said to all the animals and birds around her, "is sharing food."

One by one, the mice and doves, the voles and hedgehogs, and even the rats sat down ... and they listened.

Our books are tested
for children and young people by
children and young people.

Thanks to everyone who consulted on
a manuscript for their time and effort in
helping us to make our books better
for our readers.